MON DOMANI
"The Mother World"

SALASSANDRA
"Mystic's Moon"

MOON YATTA
"The Superpower"

GRIMBO (E)
"Moss Ocean"

The Praise for 5Worlds Is Out of This World!

A New York Public Library Top Ten Best Books for Kids Selection

A *Publishers Weekly* Best Summer Book

A Junior Library Guild Selection

"A bang-zoom start to a series
that promises to be epic in both the classical
and internet senses of the word."
—*The New York Times Book Review*

"Sensitive writing, gorgeous artwork, and riveting plot."
—*Booklist*, **Starred Review**

"A dazzling interplanetary fantasy . . . that will easily appeal to
fans of *Naruto* or *Avatar: The Last Airbender*."
—*Publishers Weekly*, **Starred Review**

"Exquisitely imagined. . . . For kids who love fantasy and other-world adventures,
and for any fans of graphic novels, this book is a must-read."
—**R. J. Palacio, #1** *New York Times* **bestselling author of** *Wonder*

"Epic action, adventure, and mystery will draw you in,
but the heartfelt characters and their seemingly impossible journey
will keep you turning the pages."
—**Lisa Yee, author of the DC Super Hero Girls™ series**

"This stellar team has created a gorgeous and entrancing world like no other!"
—**Noelle Stevenson,** *New York Times*
bestselling author of *Nimona*

5 Worlds

BOOK 2

THE COBALT PRINCE

Mark
SIEGEL

Alexis
SIEGEL

Xanthe
BOUMA

Boya
SUN

Matt
ROCKEFELLER

Random House ⌂ New York

"Moons become wet and grow into planets.
Planets become bright and grow into suns.
Suns give and give and join the stars.
And stars . . . what are stars?"

    —FROM MASTER ZELLE'S *THE BALLAD OF THE FIVE BEACONS*

SISTERS ARE FOREVER

THE FLYING FORTRESS

2

10

14

I'VE HEARD MUCH ABOUT YOU! NOW YOUR *REAL TRAINING* BEGINS, *JESSA LEE.*

OR SHALL WE FIND YOU A *TOKI NAME?*

I WOULD BE HONORED, YOUR HIGHNESS!

Z-Z-Z-AAAAₐₐ~

THE COUNCIL IS READY TO SEE YOU... DO BE PATIENT AND RESPECTFUL IN YOUR ANSWERS.

I *HAVE* BEEN PATIENT, *RONAK!*

WHY AM I STILL HERE? AREN'T THEY SENDING ME BACK TO *MON DOMANI?*

I'M AS PUZZLED AS YOU ARE.

DID YOU OR DID YOU NOT FAIL TO PREVENT THE LIGHTING OF MON DOMANI'S BEACON?

THE WHEREABOUTS OF HIS COBALT HIGHNESS ARE *NONE OF YOUR CONCERN.*

HIS HIGHNESS HIMSELF ASSURED ME THAT *THE QUEEN'S BONES WERE TO BE TAKEN DIRECTLY TO THE FLYING FORTRESS. WHAT HAPPENED TO THEM?*

JESSA ZAYD, BE WARNED. YOU ARE IN NO POSITION TO MAKE DEMANDS!

WILL YOU AT LEAST TELL ME *WHAT HAPPENED TO MY SISTER* AFTER THE LIGHTING OF THE BEACON? *SURELY SHE WAS FOUND?*

THAT IS NOT INFORMATION THIS COUNCIL SEES FIT TO SHARE. *THIS YOUNG COMMANDER FORGETS HER PLACE.*

HER FEELINGS GOT THE BETTER OF HER.

TOO MUCH PRESSURE FOR THE YOUNG LADY.

BUT OUR MISSION ON **MON DOMANI** HAS ONLY JUST BEGUN--

WE TAUGHT MON DOMANI A LESSON.

...BUT SHE IS SUFFERING FROM **COMBAT FATIGUE.** WE RECOMMEND A TEMPORARY LEAVE FOR REST AND RECUPERATION.

BUT--

THE PRINCE IS SATISFIED THAT OUR MISSION WAS **ACCOMPLISHED.** THE COUNCIL RECOGNIZES THE COMMANDER'S GOOD WORK...

THAT WAS MY HEARING?!

AFTER ALL I HAVE DONE FOR OUR PRINCE AND OUR CAUSE?

WE'VE BEEN HERE TWO DAYS!

THE COUNCIL ONLY HEARS MATTERS OF HIGH IMPORTANCE.

OUR CHILDREN ARE MISSING! THAT IS A MATTER OF HIGH IMPORTANCE!!

WE'LL GET ANSWERS, *SALDA.* I'LL WRITE ANOTHER PETITION FOR YOU. THEY HAVE TO RESPOND EVENTUALLY.

≑SOB!≑ BLESS YOU, *ELON.*

SO YOU'VE COME DOWN FROM THE FLYING FORTRESS.

MASTER ELON, I'M SO--

YOU'VE UNDERSTOOD A THING OR TWO, HAVE YOU?

COME INSIDE.

28

I WANTED TO COME EARLIER, *ELON,* I TRULY DID.

WHEN YOU WERE DECLARED *AN ENEMY OF THE CROWN,* THAT WAS MY FIRST THOUGHT.

BUT THE PRINCE FORBADE ANY CONTACT WITH YOU.

HMM...AND WHAT BRINGS YOU *TODAY?* LAST I HEARD, YOU WERE *A HIGH-RANKING COMMANDER.* WHAT DO YOU NEED FROM ME?

I... I HAVE TO UNDERSTAND WHAT HAPPENED TO *THE QUEEN'S BONES.*

THE QUEEN'S BONES?

YES, WE TOOK THEM FROM *THE SAND CASTLE.* I LED THE ASSAULT.

THE PRINCE WAS SUPPOSED TO BRING *THE QUEEN'S BONES* TO THE *FLYING FORTRESS...BUT THEY NEVER ARRIVED.*

AND OONA? MY BRAVE OONA. WHERE IS SHE NOW?

I SHOULD HAVE *LEFT* YOU TO YOUR TRAINING IN THE SAND CASTLE!

INSTEAD, I BROUGHT YOU RIGHT *INTO THE MIMIC'S GAME...*

MASTER ELON, WHAT ARE YOU SAYING?

THE PRINCE CHANGED. AT A CERTAIN POINT, *SOMETHING* HAPPENED TO HIM.

AND IN MY FOLLY, I SAW THE *MIMIC* EVERYWHERE-- IN THE SAND CASTLE, ON MOON YATTA, BUT NOT *RIGHT HERE AT HOME!*

SO...YOU MEAN...?

I MEAN: *THE MIMIC HAS POSSESSED THE COBALT PRINCE.*

WOULD THAT EXPLAIN WHY I HAVEN'T BEEN ABLE TO SUMMON *THE LIVING FIRE?*

IT HASN'T COME BACK, HAS IT? WHEN I FIRST MET YOU, YOU STILL HAD IT...AND WE KNOW *THE MIMIC CANNOT ABIDE THE LIVING FIRE...*

BUT YOUR SISTER LIT THE WHITE BEACON... *OONA IS THE KEY!*

I LEFT MY LITTLE OONA TO FOLLOW A LIE...!

BZZT!

COMMANDER *JESSA ZAYD,* YOUR PRESENCE HAS BEEN REQUESTED BY HIS HIGHNESS *THE COBALT PRINCE.*

BEFORE YOU ANSWER THAT CALL, I HAVE SOMETHING *IMPORTANT* TO SHOW YOU.

WATCH ME CAREFULLY.

LEARN THIS DANCE.

I'VE NEVER SEEN THAT SANDFORM! IS IT A MODEL OF THE FIVE WORLDS?

YES! THIS IS *THE COBALT KEY*... LONG *BANNED* BY THE TOKI ELDERS! BUT IT IS *INCOMPLETE!* THE MISSING PIECE OF IT IS...

fwoosh~

...THE LIVING FIRE!

BUT I *CAN'T* SUMMON IT, I TOLD YOU!

YOUR SISTER CAN!! *TRY IT WITH HER!* COMPLETE *THE DANCE*...

...AND LEARN WHAT *SECRET* HAS BEEN KEPT FROM US ALL!!

FIND OONA!!

FOR THE LATEST NEWS FROM THE **MON DOMANI CRISIS...**

...CITIZEN FEEDS ARE AT YOUR DISPOSAL IN THE STARBOARD GALLERY.

AND AFTER THE **SHOCKING** ATTACKS ON THE SAND CASTLE, MANY QUESTIONS REMAIN. **WHY DID THE TOKI ARMY DECLARE WAR ON MON DOMANI?**

AND WHO WAS **THE MYSTERIOUS SAND DANCER** WHO LIT THE WHITE BEACON? ARE WE ABOUT TO SEE THE **OTHER** BEACONS LIT TOO?

WOULD LIGHTING **MORE** BEACONS REVERSE THE **OVERHEATING** CRISIS OF OUR WORLDS?

SINCE THE **WHITE BEACON** WAS LIT, WE HAVE INDEED SEEN STRANGE NEW WEATHER PATTERNS.

AND THESE *HEAVY RAINS* WERE WELCOME ALL OVER *MON DOMANI*, IT IS TRUE. BUT AS YOU CAN SEE, *THEY HAVEN'T STOPPED!*

FLOODS ARE NOW THREATENING THE SOUTHERN CONTINENT! THE DROUGHTS ON *YATTA* ARE WORSENING! *SOME* ARE QUESTIONING THE *WISDOM* OF LIGHTING ANY BEACONS *AT ALL!*

CLEARLY THE *FIVE BEACONS* ARE MEANT TO WORK *TOGETHER.*

THAT'S THE ONLY WAY THE WORLDS WILL BE REBALANCED.

FOUR MORE BEACONS TO LIGHT, AND TIME IS RUNNING OUT. I'M GOING TO NEED *HELP.*

WE WILL HELP, *OONA!* BUT YOU'RE THE ONLY ONE WHO HAS *THE LIVING FIRE!*

NOT THE *ONLY ONE*, AN TZU. THERE WAS ANOTHER...*VECTOR SANDERSON.* MAYBE THERE ARE MORE OF US.

THE BEACONS MUST BE LIT. THE WORLDS DEPEND ON IT.

DO WE KNOW HOW TO DO THAT?

NO, BUT WE DIDN'T KNOW HOW TO LIGHT *THE WHITE BEACON* EITHER. REMEMBER WHAT *MEADOW* SAID...

BLOOP

"*THE SAND LIVES, THE SAND KNOWS.*"

BLOOP

WE HAVE TO GET TO THE RIGHT PLACE, WHERE THE *SAND* CAN GUIDE US.

PRRR...

I JUST WISH IT WOULD GUIDE US *AWAY FROM THE TOKI...* MAYBE *THE BLUE-SKINS* AND THE MIMIC DESERVE EACH OTHER!

NOT ALL *TOKI* ARE BAD, *AN TZU!* *VECTOR SANDERSON* IS TOKI, AND HE WAS TRYING TO LIGHT THE WHITE BEACON! HE IS THEIR GREATEST SAND DANCER! *I MAY NEED HIS HELP TO LIGHT THE BLUE BEACON!*

THE *TOKI* TOOK EVERYTHING FROM US! THEY NEARLY DESTROYED OUR HOME WORLD!

THE MIMIC ISN'T ONLY ON TOKI. *IT'S ALL OVER THE FIVE WORLDS.*

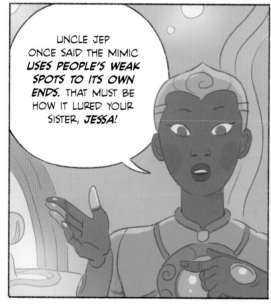

UNCLE JEP ONCE SAID THE MIMIC *USES PEOPLE'S WEAK SPOTS TO ITS OWN ENDS.* THAT MUST BE HOW IT LURED YOUR SISTER, *JESSA!*

YES, IT MIGHT BE....*THE TOKI TURNED HER INTO ONE OF THEM.*

HOW IS THAT EVEN POSSIBLE?

"NANO-GENETIC ALTERATIONS," THEY CALL IT. BUT I NEVER HEARD OF PEOPLE TAKING IT *THAT* FAR.

THEY MADE HER *BLUE!*

UGH!

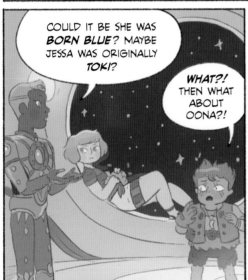

COULD IT BE SHE WAS *BORN BLUE?* MAYBE JESSA WAS ORIGINALLY *TOKI?*

WHAT?! THEN WHAT ABOUT OONA?!

NO, NO, WE REALLY *ARE* SISTERS. DEAN PLUMB ADOPTED US AND HE ALWAYS SAID SO.

HA! THIS OFF-WORLD TRAVEL IS *FRYING YOUR CIRCUITRY,* JAX!

I WONDER IF IT'S TOO LATE TO SAVE JESSA.

41

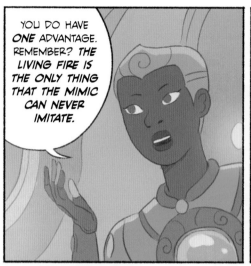

YOU DO HAVE *ONE* ADVANTAGE. REMEMBER? *THE LIVING FIRE IS THE ONLY THING THAT THE MIMIC CAN NEVER IMITATE.*

THAT'S NOT MY *ONLY* ADVANTAGE. I HAVE BOTH OF YOU WITH ME! IF WE STICK TOGETHER, THE MIMIC *DOESN'T STAND A CHANCE!*

YES, BUT FOR THAT WE HAVE TO CURE *AN TZU'S ILLNESS.* PERHAPS *A SKILLED HEALER ON TOKI?*

MIND YOUR OWN BUSINESS, BOT BOY!

COULD YOU STOP TALKING TO JAX LIKE THAT?

LOOK, I KNOW IT'S WEIRD HE'S A...A...

AN ANDROID.

...AN ANDROID.

BUT HE'S ALSO OUR *FRIEND.* I COULDN'T HAVE LIT THE BEACON WITHOUT HIM. OR YOU.

IT'S NOT YOUR FAULT, *AN TZU.* YOU ADMIRED ME AS A STARBALL PLAYER. AND YOUR TRUST WAS *BETRAYED.*

. . .

THAT MADE YOU FEEL WHAT HUMANS CALL *DISAPPOINTMENT.* I UNDERSTAND. I WISH I COULD *FEEL* IT WITH YOU. LIKE SO MANY OTHER THINGS.

BUT, AN TZU, YOU HAVE TO SEE THAT JAX IS RIGHT: YOU *NEED TO TELL US* WHAT'S HAPPENING WITH YOUR *VANISHING ILLNESS.*

IT'S NOT GOOD...

WE LEARNED SOME ANCIENT HEALING DANCES AT THE SAND CASTLE...

THIS IS MUCH WORSE THAN WHEN WE LEFT!

IT'S SPEEDING UP!!

CAN'T HURT TO TRY.

ESTEEMED PASSENGERS, THE CAPTAINS OF THE SHIP WOULD BE HONORED IF YOU WOULD JOIN THEM FOR TEA. KINDLY FOLLOW ME.

PUT THE FLOWFLEURS BACK ON!

WELCOME, DEAR GUESTS! WE ARE EXCITED TO MEET YOU. WE DON'T OFTEN GET **MON DOMANI PLANT PEOPLE** ABOARD, DO WE?

WHY, NO, IT'S DOWNRIGHT RARE. THEN AGAIN, CIRCUMSTANCES ON **MON DOMANI** ARE...SO TROUBLED.

TELL ME, THIS BUSINESS ON *TOKI*--COULD IT HAVE *SOMETHING* TO DO WITH THE WORK OF *THE LIGHTER OF BEACONS*?

. . .

SHE MEANS *THE CHOSEN ONE* WHOSE *LIVING FIRE* SOMETIMES POKES THROUGH A *FLOWFLEUR DISGUISE.*

⇒SHUTTLE PREPARING TO DOCK⇐

YAY! JUST ONE MORE TO GO!

I'VE RUN OUT OF POWER.

HE HAS US ON TARGET LOCK. ONLY ONE OPTION LEFT.

WHAT ARE YOU DOING, JAX?

SHLORP!

OONA, SWERVE!

JAX!!!

FWOOOO

WHO SENT YOU?!

IT WAS AN ACCIDENT!

OUR POD WAS FIRED ON BY TOKI SHIPS!

WHAT TOKI SHIPS?!

THE TOKI WERE AFTER OONA BECAUSE **SHE'S THE ONE WHO LIT THE BEACON!**

ENOUGH LIES!!

OOOF!!

LOOK! IT ISN'T RUNNING AWAY!

CATCH IT!!

IT'S GOING TO THE GIRL!

IT SINGS TO HER!

THE SACRED OIL IS ALIVE! AND WE'VE BEEN BURNING IT!!

LIAR!!

I QUIT!

HFF!

YOU MADE US BURN A HOLY BEING!

thok

thok

AND DON'T COME BACK!

HEY, DO YOU HAVE A NAME?

RAM SAM SAM?

IS IT *TRUE?* DID SHE REALLY LIGHT THE WHITE BEACON?

YES!

CAN YOU PLEASE HELP US? OUR SHIP WAS SHOT DOWN. WE NEED TO FIND OUR FRIEND.

THE CRASH SITE SHOULDN'T BE FAR.

IT WOULD BE AN HONOR TO HELP! I CAN LEAD YOU THROUGH THE MOUNTAIN PASS.

FOLLOW ME.

RAM SAM SAM, SALASSANDRA IS YOUR HOME, ISN'T IT?

WE'RE HEADING *OFF-WORLD*, SO YOU MAY NOT WANT TO FOLLOW US...

...OR YOU CAN COME ALONG, IF YOU WANT.

JAX...

BWEE—

WELCOME!

HOW CAN OUR HUMBLE SHOP CATER TO YOUR RELIGIOUS NEEDS? PILGRIM BELLS? WARD-OFF SPELLS? A TREE-TALKER STAFF? OR PERHAPS A LUCKY STARDUST-BUNNY?

WE CAN CERTAINLY PROVIDE IT ALL! LET'S START WITH *GARMENTS!* ONE MOMENT, PLEASE...

WE NEED PASSAGE TO *MOON TOKI.* AND SOME SIMPLE TRAVELING CLOTHES. WE HAVE *DOMANI* CREDITS.

THEY'RE IN O'ZIRG'S!! IN HERE!!

THE TEMPLE DESTROYERS!! THEY'RE IN THERE!!

ALL OF YOU, INTO THE CHANGING ROOM! NOW!!

FWP

WE'RE TRAPPED!!

FOOOOM

THAT'S FROM THE FLITORI!!

OH NO!!

SLP

ALMOST GOT THEM... ALMOST...

SLORP

BWOM-

YOU WERE ABOUT TO HAND US OVER TO THE *TOKI!* HE *SAVED US!*

YOUR FRIEND THE *STARBALL PLAYER* DIDN'T MAKE IT, DID HE?

TO THE TOKI?? CERTAINLY NOT!

SO WHAT DO YOU WANT?

WE'RE HERE TO HELP!

WHY ARE WE TRAPPED, THEN?

WE NEED TO KNOW YOU WON'T DO ANYTHING STUPID.

POP

>POP<

YOU'RE LUCKY YOU FOUND *O'ZIRG.*

HE CALLED US. IF IT WASN'T FOR US, YOU'D BE IN A *SALASSI* PRISON RIGHT NOW!

LIKE O'ZIRG, WE BELONG TO *THE ORDER OF THE QUEEN'S ARM.*

AS IN *THE GREAT QUEEN'S* ARM?

THE ARM THAT HOLDS DOWN *THE MIMIC'S HEART?*

YES.

THE ORDER HAS BEEN FIGHTING THE MIMIC FOR CENTURIES.

WE MONITOR ITS ACTIVITY IN ALL THE WORLDS.

WHERE IS IT?

BOOP!

IN MANY POSITIONS OF POWER AND INFLUENCE.

HUH?! *HOW MANY* MIMICS ARE THERE?!

WE BELIEVE THERE'S *A CENTRAL ENTITY...*

...BUT IT *MULTIPLIES* THROUGH THE PEOPLE WHO OFFER IT A GOOD *HOME.*

THERE IS STILL *MUCH* WE DON'T UNDERSTAND ABOUT IT.

WE SEE *EVIDENCE* OF IT EVERYWHERE, THOUGH.

WHAT IT WANTS ABOVE ALL IS *TO FREE ITS IMPRISONED HEART* FROM *ATBAL-BALAK.*

ATBAL-BALAK!

JAX'S UNCLE SAID YOU'D FIND ANSWERS *THERE!*

THAT'S WHERE *THE QUEEN'S MISSING ARM* VANISHED INTO THE GROUND, GRIPPING *THE MIMIC'S HEART.*

LONG AGO.

IT'S A *TOXIC WASTELAND* NOW.

THAT'S WHERE I NEED TO GO.

Chapter 4

SHADOWS OF ATBAL-BALAK

MAYBE TODAY?

STILL RED!

DIP

CLINK

HOW ABOUT THE AIR?

FWP *FWP* *FWP* *FWP*

FWP *FWP* *FWP*

STSSS *STSSS* *FWP* *STSSS* *FWP*

STILL TOXIC.

RIGHT ON TIME.

THEY BROUGHT THE SAND DANCER...

...TO THIS DEADLY WASTELAND.

VOOOM

LET'S HAVE A LOOK AT THIS *LIGHTER OF BEACONS.*

O'ZIRG?

HE'S SAFE.

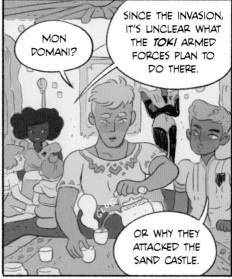

MON DOMANI?

SINCE THE INVASION, IT'S UNCLEAR WHAT THE *TOKI* ARMED FORCES PLAN TO DO THERE.

OR WHY THEY ATTACKED THE SAND CASTLE.

THEY DESTROYED THE SAND CASTLE!

BUT HOW? THAT CASTLE WAS PROTECTED BY *THE BONES OF THE GREAT QUEEN.*

THE TOKI STOLE THEM.

WHAT? OH NO...

NO...

NO...

NO!

CRASH!!

LOOK AT THIS MAP OF **ATBAL-BALAK.** I KNEW SOMETHING HAD CHANGED.

ROYAL SHIPS HAVE BEEN COMING AND GOING FROM UP HERE...

NOW I KNOW WHY!

SO YOU THINK THEY BROUGHT THE BONES **HERE?**

WHAT IS THIS PLACE?

OVER HERE IS THE TOXIC WASTELAND. RIGHT THERE, THE RUINS OF THE **NANOTEX** MINE.

ELITE TROOPS AND THE COBALT **ROYAL SHUTTLE** ITSELF ARE HERE AND HERE.

AND DOWN THERE...IS **THE MIMIC'S HEART,** TRAPPED IN THE GRIP OF **THE QUEEN'S HAND!**

THEY WANT TO USE THE QUEEN'S BONES TO RELEASE THE MIMIC'S HEART.

YES.

AND AGAINST THE CRATER'S EDGE HERE...

...IS SOME KIND OF **PRISON CAMP.**

A PRISON CAMP? **THAT'S** WHERE THEY TOOK THE **MON DOMANI** SAND DANCERS! I HAVE TO GET THEM OUT!

TAKE ME THERE!

94

IT'S A MIRACLE *OONA* MANAGED TO LIGHT THE WHITE BEACON *BY HERSELF!*

KEEP YOUR VOICE DOWN, VECTOR.

IF ONLY WE COULD GET OUT OF HERE TO HELP HER!

OONA, HOW DID YOU COME TO POSSESS *THE LIVING FIRE?*

I DON'T KNOW...

MY SISTER COULD PRODUCE IT. *VECTOR* DID, TOO.

WHAT IS *THE ORDER OF THE QUEEN'S ARM* REALLY ABOUT, MAGDA?

THE ORDER WAS **CREATED** TO PREVENT THE **MIMIC** FROM EVER REGAINING ITS HEART!

BUT WE'VE BEEN **DECIMATED.** WE'RE A SHADOW OF WHAT WE ONCE WERE.

AND NOW THE **MIMIC** IS BACK, WITH THE QUEEN'S BONES...

BUT YOU ARE HERE, **CARRIER OF THE LIVING FIRE...**

Chapter 5
CAUGHT IN A STORM

AS THEIR DRILLS NEARED THE IMPRISONED HEART, THERE WAS AN EQUIPMENT MELTDOWN, AND *A GREAT DISASTER.*

A POISONOUS *NANO-CLOUD* SPREAD OVER THE VALLEY. IT IS *A PLACE OF DEATH* TO THIS DAY.

THEN THE EVENTS WERE *COVERED UP,* AND *THE VERY NAME OF ATBAL-BALAK* WAS REMOVED FROM OFFICIAL MAPS.

FOR A SHORT TIME, THOUGH, MANY SCIENTISTS AND HEALERS *TRIED* TO HELP--*ESPECIALLY THE SICK CHILDREN.* BUT THE RESCUERS THEMSELVES OFTEN BECAME *POISONED* FROM EXPOSURE.

OF ALL THE MEMBERS OF THE ORDER AND THEIR FAMILIES, WE WERE THE HANDFUL WHO SURVIVED.

THERE WERE *THREE LITTLE CHILDREN* AMONG US. WITH STRANGE ABILITIES.

WHAT STRANGE ABILITIES?

I DON'T KNOW. THEY DISAPPEARED.... SOME SAY THE *SAND DANCERS* TOOK THEM FOR THEIR SCHOOLS.

THE LAST FEW OF US STAYED BEHIND, TO GUARD THE QUEEN'S ARM FROM *THE MIMIC*--IT MUST NEVER REGAIN ITS HEART!

ITS EVIL POWER WOULD BECOME UNSTOPPABLE!

STAY CLOSE!!

MAGDA?!

GASP!

AN TZU, YOU HAVE TO STOP.

I'M NOT WITH THE *TOKI* FORCES THAT INVADED YOUR WORLD--I'VE BEEN *FIGHTING* THEM FOR YEARS. WE HAVE TO WORK TOGETHER FOR *OONA'S SAKE.*

HOW?

ONCE THE DUST STORM CLEARS, WE'LL BE ABLE TO APPROACH THE BASE AND FIND A WAY TO RESCUE *OONA.* IN THE MEANTIME, WE HAVE TO GET YOU TREATMENT.

YOU WON'T BE ABLE TO HELP HER IF YOU'RE BARELY ABLE *TO STAND ON YOUR FEET.*

HELLO, *MISS LEE.* MY APOLOGIES FOR THE HARSH WELCOME, BUT YOUR ARRIVAL WAS...

...UNANNOUNCED.

IT'S AN *HONOR* TO MEET THE GREAT *SAND DANCER* WHO LIT *THE WHITE BEACON!*

THAT WON'T BE POSSIBLE JUST YET.

ASTONISHING. I'VE NEVER SEEN A SANDSTONE THAT COMBINES *ALL FIVE SANDS.* SO THIS IS HOW YOU LIT THE BEACON?

SPARE ME THE FLATTERY, *PRINCE OF TOKI,* AND GIVE ME BACK MY *SANDSTONE.*

WHAT? WHAT DOES MY *ADOPTION* HAVE TO DO WITH--?

DID *PLUMB* EVER MENTION *ATBAL-BALAK*?

NO...

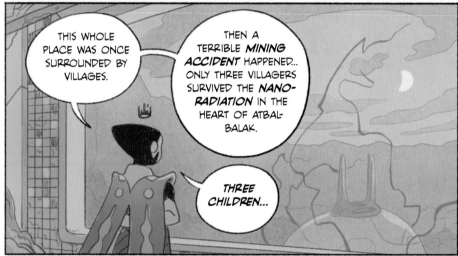

THIS WHOLE PLACE WAS ONCE SURROUNDED BY VILLAGES.

THEN A TERRIBLE *MINING ACCIDENT* HAPPENED... ONLY THREE VILLAGERS SURVIVED THE *NANO-RADIATION* IN THE HEART OF ATBAL-BALAK.

THREE CHILDREN...

THREE CHILDREN?

THREE LITTLE *TOKI* CHILDREN. THEY HAD STRANGE ABILITIES.

ARE YOU SAYING...?

I AM.

THEIR NAMES WERE *JESSA* AND *OONA*.

YOU'RE *LYING.* I AM NOT TOKI. NEITHER WAS MY SISTER UNTIL YOU GOT TO HER.

A LOT TO TAKE IN, I KNOW... OBVIOUSLY YOU DON'T REMEMBER YOUR EARLIEST DAYS. NEITHER DID *JESSA.*

HOW DID YOU TURN HER BLUE?

YOU MEAN RETURN HER TO WHO SHE TRULY WAS?

YOU AND SHE WERE *GENETICALLY ALTERED.*

WE HAVE DEVICES TO *SHUT DOWN* ANY NANO-TECHNOLOGY. IT'S AS EASY AS STEPPING THROUGH A GATE.

YOU SHOULD TRY IT FOR YOURSELF.

I WON'T.

I'M NOT ONE OF YOU! AND NEVER WILL BE!

SNAP!

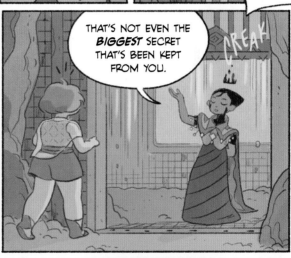

THAT'S NOT EVEN THE *BIGGEST* SECRET THAT'S BEEN KEPT FROM YOU.

CREAK

COME, *OONA LEE.* IT'S TIME YOU WERE TOLD THE TRUTH.

ABOUT THE *BEACONS.*

I HOPE A DIFFERENT FUTURE WILL SOON BE POSSIBLE WITH **MON DOMANI.**

AFTER YOU'VE **DESTROYED** EVERYTHING.

THE INVASION WAS **A LAST RESORT.** WE CAME TO IT ONLY AFTER ALL OTHER OPTIONS HAD FAILED--THE SAND DANCERS WOULD NOT LISTEN TO **REASON.**

REASON ABOUT **WHAT**?

ABOUT THEIR MAD OBSESSION WITH LIGHTING BEACONS!

WE TRIED **SO HARD** TO MAKE THEM SEE THE ERROR OF THEIR WAYS, TO NO AVAIL!

ERROR OF THEIR WAYS?

THE WORLDS ARE *OVERHEATING!* LIGHTING THE BEACONS IS *THE ONLY WAY* TO SAVE THEM!

SAVING THE FIVE WORLDS IS YOUR GOAL, THEN?

OF COURSE IT IS! THE OVERHEATING CRISIS...EVEN HERE, THERE HAVE BEEN WATER RIOTS!

THERE HAVE, INDEED.

BUT YOU WOULD HELP THE FARMERS OF TOKI BY... *TURNING MON DOMANI INTO A SUN?*

AND BURNING THIS WORLD TO ASHES?

WHAT? NO! WHAT ARE YOU TALKING ABOUT?

DEAN PLUMB NEVER TOLD YOU *WHAT THE BEACONS ARE REALLY ABOUT.*

YOU'RE RIGHT, OF COURSE. BUT WHAT WE SEE ON THE *OUTSIDE* IS NOT *THE WHOLE STORY.*

INSIDE THE BALL OF FIRE THAT WE *SEE*...

...LIES A *COOL PLANET,* A WORLD OF *LIVING SAND* ON WHICH THE *FELIDS* DEVELOPED MANY ADVANCED ARTS.

ARTS THAT SEEMED LIKE *MAGIC* TO THE MORE *PRIMITIVE* RACES THEY ENCOUNTERED IN THE UNIVERSE.

YOU SEE, THE FELIDS KNEW THAT *MOONS* CAN EVOLVE INTO *PLANETS...*

AND *PLANETS* CAN TURN INTO *SUNS.*

BUT RATHER THAN WAIT MILLIONS OF YEARS FOR THAT TO HAPPEN, THEY HAD TOOLS TO *SPEED THINGS UP.*

THEY FIRST LANDED ON *MON DOMANI.*

AND TRANSFORMED HER FOUR MOONS-- INTO *QUASI-PLANETS.*

THE *GIANT BEACONS* WERE SET UP IN PREPARATION FOR THE NEXT STAGE-- WHEN *MON DOMANI* WOULD TURN INTO...

...SUN DOMANI!

BUT THEY WERE **FORCED** TO ABANDON THEIR PROJECT WITH THE BEACONS.

BECAUSE THE MIMIC ATTACKED THE GREAT QUEEN!

OR SO THE **SAND DANCERS** WOULD HAVE YOU BELIEVE! THE TRUTH IS, THE PEOPLE OF THE FIVE WORLDS **ROSE UP AGAINST THE FELIDS!**

BECAUSE HUMANS REALIZED THAT THE **FELIDS CARED ONLY FOR MON DOMANI,** AND WERE PREPARED TO DESTROY THE OTHER WORLDS!

THEY WOULDN'T HAVE...

THE OTHER WORLDS WERE NOTHING MORE THAN TEMPORARY FARMS FOR THEIR LITTLE EXPERIMENT!

AND NOW YOU HAVE FOOLS TINKERING WITH TECHNOLOGY THAT IS BEYOND THEM.

BUT WHAT ABOUT *THE PEOPLE* WHOSE HOME WORLDS WILL BE *INCINERATED?*

ARE YOU SURE YOU WANT TO LIGHT ANY MORE BEACONS?

IF THAT WAS REALLY THE PURPOSE OF THE BEACONS, THE GREAT SAND DANCERS ON MON DOMANI WOULD KNOW IT!

AND MAYBE *THEY DO.* BUT THEY DON'T WANT YOU TO KNOW *THE TRUTH.*

AND HOW DO I KNOW *YOU* TELL THE TRUTH?

TELLING YOU THE PLAIN TRUTH IS THE ONLY WAY I SEE TO END THIS TRAGIC WAR.

WHAT...?

WHAT DO YOU *WANT* WITH ME?

TOGETHER, YOU AND I CAN BRING PEACE TO THE *FIVE WORLDS.*

BUT *YOU STARTED THIS WAR!* AND YOU STOLE THE *QUEEN'S BONES* FROM US!

YES, SADLY, WE HAD TO STOP THE *SAND CASTLE'S* MISGUIDED MASTERS FROM *DESTROYING OUR WORLDS.*

THEY WERE GOING TO *MISUSE* THE GREAT POWER OF *THE QUEEN'S BONES.*

AND WHAT WOULD *YOU* USE THOSE BONES FOR?

WHAT SAY YOU, *ZAYD?* WILL SHE JOIN OUR CAUSE?

YES, YOUR HIGHNESS. MY *SISTER* WILL COME AROUND. I WILL SEE HER TONIGHT. *AND MAKE SURE OF IT.*

Chapter 7

THE SECRET OF THE BLUE BEACON

SHH!

BRRNF

HUFF...

HUFF

HUFF...

GOT TO...
...FIND...OONA...

FIND OONA...

CREEK

THNK

...

I GUESS YOU'RE HAPPY NOW.

NO.

I'M NOT.

THIS IS NOT HOW I PICTURED US MEETING AGAIN.

ALL THOSE YEARS AFTER YOU ABANDONED ME TO GO WORSHIP THAT *TOKI PRINCE OF YOURS.*

I THOUGHT *I HAD TO, OONA.* TO SAVE THE WORLDS. *TO STOP THE MIMIC.*

BUT INSTEAD, *YOU'RE HELPING THE MIMIC.* AND TRYING TO *STOP* ME FROM LIGHTING THE BEACONS.

TFF

YOU MAY BE RIGHT, OONA.

THE PRINCE THINKS I'M HERE TO *PERSUADE* YOU. BUT I'M *NOT. PLEASE* HEAR ME OUT!

SO YOU CAN *BETRAY* ME AGAIN?

GO AWAY!

DEAN PLUMB NEVER SAID YOU AND I WERE BORN *TOKI.*

NO.

WHY DIDN'T YOU JUST *TELL* ME?

I WAS SWORN TO *SECRECY* ABOUT WHERE I WAS GOING. I THOUGHT I WOULD COME BACK FOR YOU--

EXCEPT YOUR *TOKI* TEACHER HAD OTHER PLANS.

MASTER ELON MEANT WELL. HE WAS TRICKED TOO.

SO MANY LIES! THE QUEEN'S BONES WERE SUPPOSED TO GO TO THE **FLYING FORTRESS.** THE COBALT PRINCE NEVER SAID ANYTHING TO ME ABOUT A NEW **SAND CASTLE.**

THAT'S BECAUSE IT'S JUST ONE MORE LIE!

DO **YOU** KNOW WHAT THE PRINCE IS PLANNING?

HAVEN'T YOU FIGURED OUT **WHY WE ARE HERE,** IN THIS WASTELAND? NOBODY TOLD YOU **WHAT** IS BURIED DOWN THERE IN THE GROUND?

WHAT...?

THE QUEEN'S MISSING ARM.

THE MISSING ARM...?!

AND IN THE ARM'S GRIP...

...THE DARK HEART OF THE MIMIC!!

I HAVE TO STOP HIM.

I HAVE TO FIND A WAY TO GET *YOU OUT OF HERE.*

DON'T BOTHER. TELL YOUR PRINCE *I'LL DO WHAT HE WANTS.*

BUT...*OONA!* HE IS THE *MIMIC.* YOU'RE NOT SERIOUSLY PLANNING TO GO ALONG WITH HIM, ARE YOU?

I KNOW THE *SAND* CAN GUIDE ME TO DO THE RIGHT THING.

I AM ON YOUR SIDE, OONA. NOW AND FOREVER. EVEN IF YOUR PLAN SEEMS CRAZY.

EVEN IF SUCCEEDING MEANS YOU'LL CONTINUE LIGHTING *BEACONS.*

YOU BELIEVE WHAT HE SAYS ABOUT LIGHTING BEACONS? AND TURNING MON DOMANI...*INTO A SUN?!* COULDN'T THAT BE *ANOTHER ONE OF HIS LIES?*

THERE ARE MANY OLD LEGENDS AND POEMS THAT SPEAK OF *MON DOMANI TURNING INTO A SUN.*

THE PRINCE SAYS *IT WILL BURN UP THE OTHER WORLDS.* AND I BELIEVED HIM. *THAT'S WHY WE ATTACKED MON DOMANI!*

BUT HE WAS REALLY AFTER *THE QUEEN'S BONES* ALL ALONG.

TO FIND THE TRUTH...

MAYBE *"THE COBALT KEY"* HOLDS A CLUE.

I JUST SAW OLD MASTER *ELON* AGAIN...

HE TAUGHT ME A FORBIDDEN DANCE...

IT WAS INCOMPLETE. *IT NEEDS THE LIVING FIRE...*CAN YOU SUMMON IT HERE?

SHOW ME.

OH! THAT'S *MON DOMANI.*

AND *MOON YATTA.*

TOKI.

SALASSANDRA. GRIMBO (E).

THE FIRE!

foc of!

THERE IT GOES!

THE MON DOMANI RAINS!

AND ANOTHER BEACON...LOOK! IT'S SHOOTING OUT **BEAMS**...?

...TO THE **OTHER** BEACONS?!

NOW THE **BLUE BEACON OF TOKI** IS LIGHTING UP!

ZOOOOOM

OH! WHAT HAPPENED? THE MOONS ALL *MOVED AWAY!*

THAT'S IT!! LIGHTING THE BLUE BEACON CAUSES THE FOUR MOONS' *ORBITS TO EXPAND!*

THEY MOVE AWAY...FROM *MON DOMANI...?*

SO *MON DOMANI* CAN *BECOME A SUN* WITHOUT *HARMING* THE OTHER WORLDS.

AH!

THAT'S THE *MISSING PIECE! THIS* IS WHAT THE COBALT PRINCE *DOESN'T WANT ANYONE TO KNOW*...HE HAS KEPT *TOKI FEARING THE FUTURE!*

I MISSED YOU, JESSA.

RM

SM

SM.

RM

SM

SM.

WHAT'S THAT?

RAM SAM SAM!

IT'S...*A FRIEND* FROM *SALASSANDRA.* HOW DID *YOU* FIND ME?

AN TZU?!

YOU JUST GAVE ME AN IDEA.

MISS *LEE!* WHAT IS THE OUTCOME OF YOUR DELIBERATIONS?

I NEED TO KNOW MY FRIENDS HAVEN'T BEEN HARMED.

YOUR FRIENDS ARE IN FACT...

...RIGHT HERE!

VEA! VECTOR!

THEY CAN'T *SEE OR HEAR YOU,* I'M AFRAID.

THERE WILL BE TIME FOR JOYFUL REUNIONS *AFTER* YOU HAVE RAISED THE GLORIOUS *NEW SAND CASTLE.*

BLOOT

SNAP!

WILL YOU DO IT?

PROMISE TO RELEASE MY FRIENDS, AND I'LL DO MY BEST TO DANCE *THE QUEEN'S DANCE.*

YOUR FRIENDS WILL BE FREED AND WILL BE OFFERED *A PLACE OF HONOR* AT THE GREAT SAND CASTLE.

I ONLY KNOW *THE QUEEN'S DANCE* FROM SEEING *SAND PAINTINGS* AT THE ACADEMY.

WHAT IF THE DANCE *FAILS?*

IT WON'T. WE WILL GO OVER THE STEPS TOGETHER BEFORE HEADING TO *THE SITE.*

I TAKE IT *YOU ARE READY TO RETURN TO YOUR TRUE NATURE,* THEN?

PLUMB'S *ALTERATIONS* MADE ME LIVE *A LIE.*

I NEVER CHOSE THEM.

I WAS NEVER TOLD *WHAT* HAD BEEN DONE TO ME.

I WANT TO BE RID OF THEM.

SHI–ING

BUT IT WON'T HELP YOU MOVE THOSE PLANTS. THEY DON'T RECOGNIZE *OFF-WORLD TUNES.*

HOWEVER BEAUTIFUL.

YOU ARE ANGRY, LITTLE BROTHER.

YOU COME FROM ONE OF THE OTHER WORLDS?

MOTHER WORLD.

THE *BLUE-SKINS* ATTACKED US.

AND YOU'RE HERE TO ATTACK THEM BACK WITH THAT *FLUTE?*

YOU THINK THAT'S FUNNY?

HFF

HF

157

I DREAMED OF THE GODS.

I HAVE TO GET BACK TO HER!

EVEN THOUGH SHE'S...*BLUE. THAT'S* WHAT YOU'VE BEEN SAYING TO ME ALL ALONG, RIGHT, RAM SAM SAM?

NOD NOD

AND WHY ARE YOU SO MUCH SMALLER? *WHERE'S...THE REST OF YOU?*

KSH
KSH

KSH

Chapter 9
THE QUEEN'S BONES

ATBAL-BALAK,
OLD **NANOTEX**
MINING COMPLEX

ITS NAME IS *RAM SAM SAM.*

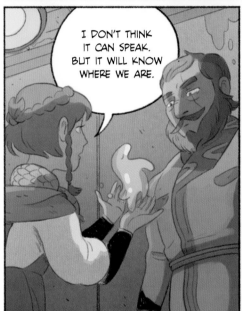

I DON'T THINK IT CAN SPEAK. BUT IT WILL KNOW WHERE WE ARE.

WATCH IT CAREFULLY, AND DO AS IT SAYS. OR *SHOWS...*

DO NOT UNDERESTIMATE THE PRINCE.

NO.

BUT *THIS TIME,* I'M NOT UNDERESTIMATING *OONA,* EITHER.

I MUST GO! SHE AND I ARE TO MEET HIM NOW.

GOOD LUCK, *RONAK.*

GOOD LUCK, *JESSA.*

AND HERE IS JESSA. THE SISTERS REUNITED!

ON WE GO, NOW, TO THE HEART OF *ATBAL-BALAK!* LET'S NOT KEEP THE GREAT QUEEN WAITING, SHALL WE?

HER *BONES* ARE THERE ALREADY.

MEANWHILE...

AND ON THE OUTER EDGE OF ATBAL-BALAK...

THAT'S WHERE WE NEED TO GO!

THE *PLANTS* CAN HELP US GET THERE...YOU REMEMBER THAT TUNE, *AN TZU MAN*?

I KNOW, I KNOW, *LITTLE BEING.* THAT'S WHERE WE NEED TO GO.

BUT WE CAN'T SET FOOT IN THIS *TOXIC WASTELAND.*

IT WOULD KILL US ALL IN A SECOND.

?!

THIS PLACE LOOKS DEADLY.

THE PLANTS CAN ABSORB THE *TOXINS.*

RRM smm!

THE GREAT SAND CASTLE OF THE NEW ERA WILL RISE HERE, *OONA.*

AND YOU WILL BE ITS FOUNDER!

THE *MIMIC* HAS POSSESSED THE *COBALT PRINCE!* SOMETHING BAD IS GOING TO HAPPEN AT THE CONSTRUCTION SITE!

THE *LIGHTER OF BEACONS* IS THERE. WE NEED TO HELP HER.

OONA LEE NEEDS ALL OF US!

LEAD THE WAY!

TIME FOR ME TO LEND A HAND, OONA.

YOU LIED! YOU ARE THE MIMIC'S CREATURE!

CLEVER GIRL! BUT YOU'RE A BIT LATE...

IT'S CLOSING UP!!

WHRRRR

MUST...

...GET THROUGH...

JUMP

WHRRR

THMP!

THUD!!

NO!!

NO!!

OONA!!

WE'RE TOO LATE!!

SLAM!

SHE FELL!!!

WHAT'S UNDER THIS CONSTRUCTION SITE? IT MUST CONNECT TO THE OLD NANOTEX MINE. WE NEED A MAP OF THE TUNNELS!

I KNOW WHO CAN GUIDE US INTO THE MINE!

RAM SAM SAM, WHERE'S MAGDA?

MAGDA, *HELP!* OONA FELL!!

I *SAW!* I *KNOW* WHERE THE PRINCE IS HEADED. WE HAVE TO GO DOWN THE SHAFT OF THE OLD MINE!

WE'RE GOING TO ENCOUNTER **EXTENSIVE CONTAMINATION** IN THE LOWER LEVELS. NONE OF YOU ARE PROTECTED. THE CHILDREN HAVE TO STAY UP HERE.

OONA NEEDS HELP! SHE'S ALONE AGAINST THE MIMIC. I'M COMING!

ME TOO!

WE'RE COMING TOO!

THE **PLANTS** CAN ABSORB MOST OF THE CONTAMINATION. WE'RE **WILLING** TO GO!

OKAY, THIS WAY!

MEANWHILE...

THERE MUST BE A FASTER WAY DOWN! *WE'VE GOT TO REACH OONA!!*

SSSHHAA

HUP!

BZZT

CH-DUNK

CH-DUNK

CH-DU

LEAVE MY SISTER ALONE!

JESSA!

ZAYD!
INTENT ON
JOINING YOUR
SISTER IN DEATH,
ARE YOU?

SSFF

BEGONE, MIMIC!

HALT!!

AGH... WHAT...?!

I TRAINED YOU, *JESSA*... DIDN'T YOU THINK I WOULD HAVE THE FORESIGHT TO SLIP IN A BIT OF A *FAIL-SAFE?*

BRING ME THE QUEEN'S BONES.

NO, JESSA, DON'T!!

URGL GLR

YOU THINK YOU'VE DEFEATED ME, SAND DANCER?

THIS IS NOTHING TO ME. THAT BODY WAS *NOTHING.*

YOU ARE NOTHING. AND I AM EVERYWHERE.

EVERYWHERE YOU'LL GO-- URG GLRG

gurgle

glop

AAMLAK CITY, THE FLYING FORTRESS

OONA, WHAT I DID TO YOU AND JESSA WAS TERRIBLY WRONG. I AM SO VERY SORRY.

DEAN PLUMB, HOW COULD YOU NOT TELL US THAT YOU'D HAD US *ALTERED*?

I WAS A FOOL NOT TO TRUST YOU.

BUT THERE WAS SO MUCH ANGER AMONG THE *TOKI* AFTER THEIR DEFEAT IN *THE FIVE WORLDS WAR.*

I WAS AFRAID THE *MIMIC* WOULD EXPLOIT IT AND SPREAD ITS INFLUENCE ON TOKI.

YOU WEREN'T ENTIRELY WRONG.

SO WHEN I HEARD THAT THREE YOUNG KIDS AT *ATBAL-BALAK* HAD MANIFESTED *THE LIVING FIRE...*

...I THOUGHT THOSE POWERS SHOULD SERVE *THE SAND CASTLE,* RATHER THAN *TOKI* UNDER THE MIMIC'S SWAY.

YOU DID THAT THROUGH *DECEPTION.* YOU CHANGED *EVERY CELL* IN OUR BODIES.

YOU WIPED OUR MEMORIES OF BEING BLUE!

WHAT I DID WAS UNFORGIVABLE.

YOU AND JESSA SHOULD HAVE GROWN UP AS YOUR OWN BEAUTIFUL *TOKI* SELVES, LIKE *VECTOR.* THAT IS WHAT I PLAN TO TELL THE NEW TOKI AUTHORITIES...

AND I WILL SUBMIT TO WHATEVER *PUNISHMENT* THEY SEE FIT TO GIVE ME FOR MY CRIME.

PUNISHMENT FOR YOUR CRIME? DEAN PLUMB, WHAT ARE YOU TALKING ABOUT?

YES, A LONG SENTENCE IN A *TOKI* PRISON WILL GIVE ME PLENTY OF TIME TO REFLECT ON ALL THE *HARM* I HAVE CAUSED.

HAVE YOU FORGOTTEN THAT THE WORLDS ARE FACING *EXTINCTION?* THAT THE *MIMIC* IS FAR FROM DEFEATED?

NO...

THAT'S CERTAINLY TRUE, BUT...

MAGDA SAYS IT WILL TAKE *A LONG TIME* FOR THE KIDNAPPED CHILDREN TO BE TRULY RID OF THE *MIMIC'S INFLUENCE* IN THEM.

WELL, THAT SOUNDS LIKE EXACTLY THE RIGHT SENTENCE FOR YOU, DEAN PLUMB-- *SAVING* THOSE CHILDREN...

...BY *TEACHING* THEM THE TRUE SAND DANCING ARTS.

BUT THE SAND CASTLE--

...WAS DESTROYED.

SO YOU'LL HAVE TO TAKE THE *QUEEN'S BONES* BACK TO *MON DOMANI* AND BUILD A NEW SAND DANCING ACADEMY. SOUNDS LIKE MANY YEARS' HARD LABOR TO ME!!

YOU TRULY ARE EXTRAORDINARY, *OONA, LIGHTER OF THE BEACONS!*

WELL, *YOU* TRAINED ME.

DEAN PLUMB, HAVE YOU EVER HEARD OF *STAR-LEVEL DANCING?*

STAR-LEVEL...

YES, IT'S MENTIONED IN ANCIENT CARVINGS, BUT I'VE NEVER REACHED THAT LEVEL MYSELF. THE *ONLY KNOWN PRACTITIONER OF IT,* WELL...

...EVERYONE USED TO LAUGH AT HER. SAID SHE WAS A *FAKE,* A *TRICKSTER.*

MASTER ZELLE ON *MOON YATTA.*

SOME OF US THOUGHT SHE WAS *NO FOOL!* SHE WAS SAID TO *APPEAR AND DISAPPEAR* MYSTERIOUSLY.

LAST I HEARD, SHE AND A SMALL BAND OF DISCIPLES...

...HAD RETREATED TO THE CAVES OF THE *RUBY DESERT.*

VECTOR! OR IS IT **YOUR COBALT HIGHNESS** NOW?

NO TEASING, OONA. **RONAK** AND **MAGDA** PRETTY MUCH SPRANG IT ON ME.

SPRANG IT ON YOU?

YES, AT THE FIRST MEETING OF THE **INTERIM HIGH COUNCIL,** NAMING ME THE NEW PRINCE BEFORE ANYTHING ELSE...

THEN **THORN** AND **MASTER ELON** AND THE OTHERS ALL AGREED.

WHAT, AND **YOU** DIDN'T?

I WASN'T SURE WE **NEEDED** A PRINCE. BUT EVERYONE SAYS THIS WILL HELP **REBUILD THE WORLD.**

THERE'S SO MUCH TO REPAIR AND REBALANCE, TO COUNTERACT THE MIMIC'S POISON-- IN THOSE POOR CHILDREN, IN *ATBAL-BALAK...*

HERE AT THE FORTRESS. *IT WILL TAKE EVERYONE'S HELP.*

YOU LOOK NICE AS A TOKI, OONA.

IS IT TRUE *THORN* IS OVERSEEING THE DECONTAMINATION OF *ATBAL-BALAK?*

YES. SHE AND HER FELLOW *PLANT PEOPLE* COULD'VE HELPED MANY YEARS AGO, BUT THEY WERE NEVER CONSULTED! A LOT HAS BEEN *WRONG* FOR A LONG TIME HERE.

CAN YOU TAKE TIME OUT OF YOUR BUSY SCHEDULE TO HELP ME LIGHT *THE BLUE BEACON?*

WHY, *YES!* WE *WILL* END UP DOING A BEACON DANCE TOGETHER AFTER ALL. WE CAN DO IT RIGHT AFTER THE *SAND CLEANSING* CEREMONY!

SAH·FFF

SAND CLEANSING?

YES, AN TZU'S FRIEND *ANSELKA* HAS AGREED TO HELP US RID *TOKI* SAND OF THOSE *NANO-PARTICLES* THAT MADE IT DESTRUCTIVE AND DANGEROUS.

WE WANT OUR SAND TO BE A TOOL OF *LEARNING* AND *HEALING,* NOT A WEAPON.

YOU'RE GROWING INTO THIS *ROYAL LEADERSHIP* THING, VECTOR!

"THE SAND LIVES, THE SAND KNOWS." AND THE ROYAL LEADER LISTENS.

NOW IF THE SAND CAN JUST *GUIDE US TO THE LIGHTING OF THE BEACON...*

THE NEW PRINCE IS YOUNG. HE WILL MAKE MISTAKES.

AND WHEN HE DOES, WE WILL BE READY.

SSSHH

THE CROWDS ARE CHEERING HIM TODAY.

BUT *OUR POWERFUL FRIENDS* ON *MOON YATTA* WILL SUPPORT US WHEN THE TIME COMES.

WHY WON'T IT LIGHT?! ONCE MORE!

YOU HAVE *THE LIVING FIRE* AND *THE SAND WARRIOR!* JUST TRY AGAIN!

WHAT DID I DO WRONG? WHY WON'T IT LIGHT?

THE BLUE BEACON ISN'T READY TO BE LIT!

?!

?

THAT VOICE...?

JAX AMBOY!!

JAX!! YOU'RE ALIVE!

SORRY I WASN'T AROUND TO HELP. LOOKS LIKE YOU'VE BEEN BUSY ENDING A WAR.

YES. THE NEW COBALT PRINCE IS OUR *FRIEND*.

BUT IT SEEMS I *CAN'T* LIGHT ANY MORE *BEACONS*. HE AND I TRIED, BUT IT DIDN'T HAPPEN.

THAT'S BECAUSE YOU *DON'T* LIGHT THE *BLUE* BEACON NEXT.

WHAT?

I'VE *DECRYPTED* MY UNCLE JEP'S ARCHIVE.

HE BELIEVED THERE'S A **SEQUENCE** TO LIGHTING THE BEACONS.

IT WAS RIGHT HERE ALL ALONG, ON MY NEW HAND: **WHITE, RED, BLUE, YELLOW, GREEN.**

SO...AFTER THE **WHITE** BEACON, **RED** IS NEXT?

WE NEED TO GO TO **MOON YATTA!**

THE THREE CAPTAINS OF THE *FLITORI* WILL BE GLAD TO SEE YOU AGAIN!

OFF YOU GO, THEN, *LIGHTER OF BEACONS!*

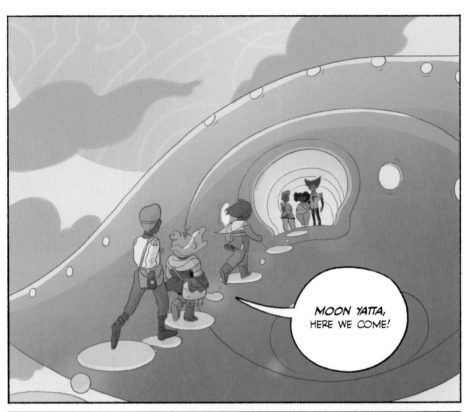

MOON YATTA, HERE WE COME!

MY DAD ALWAYS **DREAMED** OF GOING THERE ONE DAY. HE USED TO SING, *"O FAIR YATTA, HOPE OF THE FIVE WORLDS..."*

"...MOON OF FREEDOM, AND JUSTICE AND OPPORTUNITY..."

TO BE CONTINUED IN 5W3: *THE RED MAZE*

To Milo—MS

To Harvey and Milo—AS

To Adeetje—XB

To Gram—MR

To the Macfarlane family—BS

ACKNOWLEDGMENTS

Tanya McKinnon, always

Our amazing Random House team:
Michelle Nagler, Chelsea Eberly, Elizabeth Tardiff, Kelly McGauley, Aisha Cloud,
Joshua Redlich, Kim Lauber, Alison Kolani, Dominique Cimina, Lisa Nadel,
Adrienne Waintraub, Laura Antonacci, John Adamo, Jocelyn Lange, Joe English,
Mallory Loehr, Barbara Marcus

+ Special thanks for added help, friendship & magic:
Siena Siegel, Sonia Siegel, Shudan Yeh, Felix Siegel, Julien & Clio Siegel,
Julie Sandfort, Viviana Simon, Hilde McKinnon, Sam Dutter, Cynthia Cheng

And Lisa Yee, Kazu Kibuishi, Noelle Stevenson, Gene Luen Yang,
Vera Brosgol, Lee Wade, Sam Bosma, Kali Ciesemier

And for lighting the way to beloved new worlds:
Ursula K. LeGuin, Hayao Miyazaki, Neil Gaiman

Copyright © 2018 by Antzu Pantzu, LLC

All rights reserved. Published in the United States by Random House Children's Books, a division of Penguin Random House LLC, New York.

Random House and the colophon are registered trademarks of Penguin Random House LLC.

Visit us on the Web! rhcbooks.com

Educators and librarians, for a variety of teaching tools, visit us at RHTeachersLibrarians.com

Library of Congress Cataloging-in-Publication Data
Names: Siegel, Mark, 1967– , author. | Siegel, Alexis, author. | Bouma, Xanthe, illustrator. |
Rockefeller, Matt, illustrator. | Sun, Boya, illustrator.
Title: The cobalt prince / Mark Siegel, Alexis Siegel ;
illustrated by Xanthe Bouma, Matt Rockefeller, and Boya Sun.
Description: First edition. | New York : Random House, [2018] | Series: 5 worlds ; book 2 |
Summary: Sisters Jessa and Oona, and new friend Ram Sam Sam, try to stop the Cobalt Prince
from Toki, who orders a strike on Mon Domani, starting a new worlds war.
Identifiers: LCCN 2017026243 | ISBN 978-1-101-93589-7 (hardcover) | ISBN 978-1-101-93591-0 (pbk.) |
ISBN 978-1-101-93605-4 (ebook) | ISBN 978-1-101-93590-3 (lib. bdg.)
Subjects: LCSH: Graphic novels. | CYAC: Graphic novels. | Heroes—Fiction. | Adventure and adventurers—
Fiction. | Science fiction.
Classification: LCC PZ7.7.S4825 Cob 2018 | DDC 741.5/973—dc23

MANUFACTURED IN CHINA

10 9 8 7 6 5 4 3 2 1

First Edition

Where has Jax been? What adventures are in store? Find out in

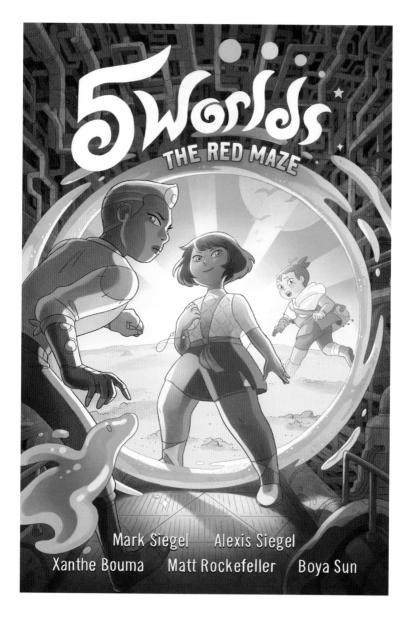

5W3:
THE RED MAZE

MARK SIEGEL has written and illustrated several award-winning picture books and graphic novels, including the *New York Times* bestseller **Sailor Twain** and **Oskar and the Eight Blessings.** He is also the editorial and creative director of First Second Books. He lives with his family in New York.

ALEXIS SIEGEL is a writer and translator based in Switzerland. He has translated a number of bestselling graphic novels, including Joann Sfar's **The Rabbi's Cat** and Pénélope Bagieu's **Exquisite Corpse** into English and Gene Luen Yang's **American Born Chinese** into French.

XANTHE BOUMA is an illustrator based in Southern California. When not working on picture books such as **Little Sid,** fashion illustration, and comics, Xanthe enjoys soaking up the beachside sun.

MATT ROCKEFELLER is an illustrator and comic artist from Tucson, Arizona. His work has appeared in a variety of formats, including book covers, animation, and picture books such as **Train, Rocket,** and **Pop!** He also illustrates the middle-grade series **The Explorers.**

BOYA SUN is an illustrator and coauthor of the graphic novel **Chasma Knights.** Originally from China, Boya has traveled from Canada to the United States and now lives in Northern California.

A Sneak Peek at the Making of 5W2
Character Development

An Tzu (Xanthe)

Early Ram Sam Sam (Mark)

More Ram Sam Sam (Xanthe)

Oona colors (Xanthe)

Young Jessa and Oona (Boya)

Magda Gadek (Matt)

Giant Chibi (Matt)

O'Zirg (Boya)

Master Elon (Boya)

Thorn (Boya)

Prince before Mimic (Xanthe)

World Building

FL'IORI ESCAPE POD

TEMPLE OF THE SINGING FLAME

Salassandra studies (Matt)

SALASSI STREET 1

SALASSI STREET 2

O'ZIRG'S SHOP

CHANGING ROOM

O'ZIRG'S SHOP, MAIN COUNTER

Toki studies (Matt)

INDOOR/OUTDOOR COURTYARDS MIX ROCK & ARCHITECTURE

NANOTEX MINE SHAFT

UNDERGROUND HOLDING AREA

MIMA'S HEART CHAMBER

HIGH COUNCIL OF TOKI

MINE ELEVATOR

DONA'S CELL

Mapping out the battle of Atbal-Balak (Matt)

TOP OF THE NANOTEX MINING SHAFT

ATBAL BALAK IMPACT CRATER

NANOTEX MINE

...and many sketchbooks more!

Discover more online!

@5WorldsTeam

POST YOUR **COSPLAY** PHOTOS
AND SHARE YOUR BEST **FAN ART**
WITH OTHER 5-WORLDERS!

F. as An Tzu

Summer Ramos

Olivia Huynh

AND STAY TUNED
FOR CONTESTS
AND SPECIAL EVENTS
ON A PLANET NEAR YOU!

Don Ahé